USBORNE FI...
Level...

USBORNE FIRST READING

The **Dinosaur**
Who Lost His **ROAR**

Russell Punter
Illustrated by Andy Elkerton

USBORNE FIRST READING

The **Castle**
That **Jack Built**

Lesley Sims

Illustrated by
Mike Gordon

USBORNE FIRST READING

**Chicken**
**Licken**

retold by
Russell Punter

Illustrated by Ann Kronheimer

USBORNE FIRST READING

The
**Three Little**
**Pigs**

retold by
Susanna Davidson
Illustrated by Georgien Overwater

# The Three Little Pigs

### Retold by
### Susanna Davidson

### Illustrated by
### Georgien Overwater

Reading Consultant: Alison Kelly
Roehampton University

Once upon a time, there were three little pigs...

Pinky,

Percy

and

Poppy.

2

They lived with their
mother in a pretty
little house.

But the little pigs grew
too big.

"We want homes of our own," they said.

So they packed their bags and waved goodbye.

"Watch out for the Big Bad Wolf," called Mother Pig.

We will!

7

The three little pigs
trotted along until...

...they met a man selling straw.

"Can I buy some straw?"
asked Pinky Pig.

"I'm going to build
a house."

Pinky Pig worked
very fast. He made
four straw walls

12

a straw roof and a
straw door.

Then he put down a
soft straw floor.

"Look at my house!"
he said. "Isn't it grand?"

Then he went inside
and shut the door.

Percy and Poppy Pig
trotted on until...

Sticks
for
sale

...they met a man
selling sticks.
"Can I buy some sticks?"
asked Percy Pig.

I'm going
to build
a house.

Sticks
for
sale

"Sticks are better
than straw."

19

Then he went inside and shut the door.

Poppy Pig trotted on until...

...she saw some bricks for sale.

"Can I buy some bricks?"
asked Poppy Pig.

"I'm going to build
a house."

Poppy Pig worked hard.

"Bricks are better than
straw," she said.

"Bricks are better
than sticks."

"But they're so heavy."

At last, the
brick house
was finished.

The next day, the Big Bad Wolf went to the straw house.

"Little pig, little pig, let
me come in," he called.

"No!" cried Pinky Pig.
"Not by the hair on my
chinny-chin-chin."

"Then I'll huff and I'll
puff and I'll blow your
house in," said the wolf.

And he huffed
and he puffed

and he blew the house in.

Pinky ran as fast as he
could to the stick house.

The wolf was just
behind him.

"Little pigs, little pigs,
let me come in," said
the wolf.

"No!" cried Percy Pig.
"Not by the hair on my
chinny-chin-chin."

"Then I'll huff and I'll puff
and I'll blow your house
in," said the wolf.

And he huffed
and he puffed

and he huffed
and he puffed

until at last he blew the house in.

Pinky and Percy ran
as fast as they could
to the brick house.

The wolf was just
behind them.

"Little pigs, little pigs, let me come in," said the wolf.

"No!" cried Poppy Pig.
"Not by the hair on my
chinny-chin-chin."

"Then I'll huff and I'll puff and I'll blow your house in," said the wolf.

And he huffed and he
puffed and he huffed

and he puffed. He huffed
and puffed until...

...he ran out of puff.
"Hee, hee, hee," laughed
the three little pigs.

"I'm coming to get you!"
cried the wolf.

He jumped onto the roof.

He slid down
the chimney

and landed *splosh*
in Poppy's cooking pot.
46

The three little pigs
slammed on the lid.

And that was the end of
the Big Bad Wolf.

*The Three Little Pigs* is a very old story. It was first written down around two hundred years ago, but people were telling it to each other long before then.

Series editor: Lesley Sims

Designed by Louise Flutter

First published in 2007 by Usborne Publishing Ltd., Usborne House, 83-85 Saffron Hill, London EC1N 8RT, England. www.usborne.com
Copyright © 2007 Usborne Publishing Ltd.

48

# USBORNE FIRST READING
## Level Four